The Hare and the Tortoise

A SIENA BOOK

Siena is an imprint of Parragon Books

Published by Parragon Book Service Ltd.
Units 13-17, Avonbridge Trading Estate,
Atlantic Road, Avonmouth, Bristol BS11 9QD

Produced by The Templar Company plc, Pippbrook Mill,
London Road, Dorking, Surrey RH4 1JE

Copyright © 1996 Parragon Book Service Limited

Designed by Mark Kingsley-Monks

Printed and bound in Italy

ISBN 0-75251-206-4

The Hare and the Tortoise

Illustrated by Lorna Hussey
Retold by Caroline Repchuk

SIENA

Once there lived a handsome
hare who was terribly proud
of himself. He was especially
proud of his strong back legs,
which helped him to run faster
than any animal he had ever met.

He would challenge any animal to a race. No matter how hard they tried, the hare would always beat them.

Now, as well as being proud, this hare also thought that he was very wise and clever, and that no-one could get the better of him. And no-one could — until one day the tortoise came crawling by.

"Ho, ho, ho," laughed the hare, as the slow old tortoise came along the road. "Hurry up, slowcoach. If you go any slower you'll stop!"

The tortoise stopped and looked at the hare.

"You can rush about if you want to, but why should I hurry?" he asked.

"I don't have time to waste," said the hare. "I'm a very important hare."

"I get where I'm going soon enough," said the tortoise. "In fact, I bet I could get anywhere faster than you!"

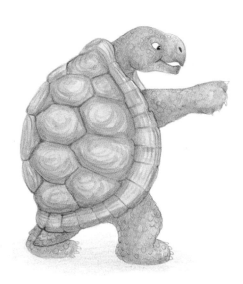

"Faster than me?" laughed the hare. "No-one can run faster than me!"

"Well, to prove it," said the tortoise, "I challenge you to a race!" And so the race was set for the very next day.

Fox was the umpire, so he fired the starting pistol and the race began. The hare was away in a flash and in no time had disappeared over the hill.

Behind him, the tortoise took slow plodding steps, keeping his eyes fixed on the road ahead.

On raced the hare, and everyone cheered as he sped by. Before long he reached the halfway mark and, thinking he had lots of time, he stopped for a nap under a tree.

Hours went by, and at last along came the tortoise. He smiled when he saw the hare fast asleep, and carried steadily on down the road.

At last the hare woke up and hurried on towards the finish line. The tortoise was nowhere to be seen.

"He's probably still at the start!" thought the hare.

As the hare raced towards the finish line he could hear everyone cheering. Then he saw the tortoise —he had just broken through the finishing tape!

As the hare puffed and panted to the end of the race, the tortoise held up the winning cup and said:

"I may be slow, but I keep my eye on the goal ahead. And let that be a lesson to you!"

Moral: Slow and steady wins the race.